# Pearlie and Jasper

## WENDY HARMER

Illustrated by Mike Zarb

and Gypsy Taylor

RANDOM HOUSE AUSTRALIA

For the beautiful Miss Rosie Riley

Random House Australia Pty Ltd
Level 3, 100 Pacific Highway, North Sydney, NSW 2060
http://www.randomhouse.com.au

Sydney   New York   Toronto
London   Auckland   Johannesburg

First published by Random House Australia 2006
Copyright © Out of Harms Way Pty Ltd 2006

National Library of Australia
Cataloguing-in-Publication Entry

    Harmer, Wendy.
    Pearlie and Jasper.

    For lower primary school aged children.
    ISBN 1 74166 011 4.

    1. Fairies – Juvenile fiction. I. Title.

    A823.3

Designed and typeset by Jobi Murphy
Printed and bound by Sing Cheong
Printing Co. Ltd, Hong Kong

20 19 18 17 16 15 14 13 12 11

It was a very cold winter afternoon in Jubilee Park. Pearlie the park fairy had made sure that everything was in its place, just right, for when the children came to play, but no-one had come to visit all day.

Pearlie looked out
from her shell on top of
the old stone fountain.
The wind gave her tiny
nose an icy nip.

'Hurrrly-burrrly, brrr,
it's chilly today!' she said.
She ducked back inside
her cosy home and
pulled her feather
curtains closed.

Pearlie was making herself a gumnut full of hot sunflower seed soup when she heard a small voice.

'H . . . h . . . hello. Is . . . is . . . th . . . th . . . there anyone home?'

She poked her head outside and there,
looking at her from under a stripy knitted hat,
was an elf.

'Hail and icicles!' exclaimed Pearlie.
'You must be freezing. Come inside
at once and warm up.'

In an instant Pearlie had tucked the elf into her favourite chair under a fluffy duck down blanket and given him the gumnut of hot soup. He drank it in one gulp. 'Oh, that was excellent. Thanks, man!' said the elf.

Pearlie thought this was an odd thing to say. After all, she wasn't a man, she was a fairy.

'My name's Jasper,' he said with a smile.

'I'm Pearlie. Welcome to my home,' she replied.

'Sweet,' said Jasper. 'You have a really cool place!'

'Oh dear,' said Pearlie. 'Would you like another blanket?'

'No, I mean your shell is lovely. You are so lucky! I wish I still had my house,' Jasper sniffed, and his blue eyes filled with tears.

'Oh dear,' said Pearlie. 'What happened?'

'My house was right up
on a high branch of a
beautiful lilly-pilly tree
in a nature strip on the
other side of the city,'
Jasper explained.

'I made it out of leaves. It was green
and soft, but really strong when the wind blew.
I made a chair from some old snail shells.
I had a cobweb hammock . . .

'But a big person came and cut down my tree
with a chainsaw to make room for a new road!'
Jasper sobbed. 'That beautiful lilly-pilly was
my best friend.'

'Roots and twigs!' thought Pearlie.
This was a very sad
tale indeed.

'Well, you must stay with me tonight and tomorrow we will find you a new house right here in Jubilee Park,' said Pearlie.

'Really? Do you mean it?' asked Jasper.

And, of course, because Pearlie was such a kind-hearted fairy, she meant every word.

'Sweet ... zzzzzz.' Jasper was so worn out he fell fast asleep in the chair.

The next morning Pearlie and Jasper saw that the sun had come out. It was a good morning to go house hunting.

Pearlie gave Jasper a woolly jumper to wear. He pulled it over his head and shook out his long tails of brown hair. Pearlie had never seen an elf with a hairdo quite like it!

'Now we must find you another tree,' said Pearlie. She thought it would be fun to have Jasper as a neighbour.

'No way,' said Jasper, shaking his head so hard his hat almost flew off. 'No more trees. I could never replace my dear lilly-pilly. Could I stay and live with you?'

'I'm sorry,' said Pearlie, 'but there's only enough room in my shell for one.' Then she had a good idea. 'Let's go and see if anyone else in the park has a room for rent.'

Pearlie and Jasper flew off. Pearlie saw that although Jasper's wings were smaller than hers, he could fly very fast.

Every now and then he did a somersault, which made her laugh.

The first place they stopped was the little
spiders' web.

'Yes, we have some room in our cobweb,'
said Sulky.

'It's very strong and sticky. You'd never fall off.'

His sister Silky agreed. 'And we can move it any time we like to be nearer the flies.'

Jasper didn't think he would like to live in a cobweb. 'I don't like flies much,' he said.

Pearlie thanked the spiders then took Jasper by the hand and they flew to the edge of the pond.

Squish, squelch, plip, plop! Four fat froggy heads poked out of the black mud.

'You couldn't find a better home for the winter than this smelly slop,' said the biggest frog.

'And in summer, we all move to our holiday houses on the lily pads. It's wet and wobbly and there are lots of delicious mosquitoes to eat,' said the smallest.

'Jump right on in!' they all sang together.

Jasper didn't think a pile of mud would make a good home either. 'I think I need somewhere nice and dry,' he said.

Pearlie agreed and then took Jasper to meet Mother Duck in the long reeds.

'WAKKA WAK! The best place in Jubilee Park is under my wings,' she squawked.

She lifted up her feathers and four little duck bills popped out and started to quack all at once.

'IT'S A BIT NOISY AND CROWDED, BUT YOU'RE VERY WELCOME!' she yelled.

Then she pecked her ducklings hard on the tops of their heads. 'Get back inside, right this minute!' she said crossly.

'I don't think there's enough room for me,' said Jasper politely. Pearlie thanked Mother Duck and off they flew to see Brush and Sugar possum in their favourite hole in a tree trunk.

'Well,' yawned Brush, 'you could move into our tree tomorrow – as long as you don't make any noise in the daytime.'

'And you don't mind us jumping about all night,' added Sugar.

Jasper shook his head. 'I like to sleep when it's dark. Thank you all the same.'

Pearlie was starting to wonder where Jasper might live. He did need a cosy house. It was a very cold day.

'Have a look around Jubilee Park and see what you can find. I'll go home and make us some hot lunch,' said Pearlie, and off she flew.

Jasper was just peeking under a park bench when who should come strolling by? It was those two bad ratbags Scrag and Mr Flea.

'Excuse me,' said Jasper. 'Do you know anyone in Jubilee Park who has a room to rent?'

'Well, well, well,' said Scrag with an evil look in his eye. 'As a matter of fact we do have a very charming little room in our delightful home we'd be glad to rent.'

'We do?' said Mr Flea. Scrag nudged him hard in his fat, flea-bitten gut.

'It's beautifully furnished, very warm and has marvellous water views,' said Scrag. 'In fact it's the perfect home for an elf such as yourself!'

'Yeah, yeah. Perfectly awful,' Mr Flea sniggered to himself.

'Hey, thanks dudes!' said Jasper who was the sort of elf who liked to trust everyone he met.

Scrag and Mr Flea took Jasper's arms and led him along the gutter to their house. It was *not* a charming spot – it was a filthy, smelly drain!

Jasper took one look and didn't like it at all. But before he could say a word the two bad ratbags pushed him inside and locked the grate.

'We won't let you out until you have cleaned up EVERYTHING!' shouted Scrag.

'Yeah! And don't forget to wash my underpants!' yelled Mr Flea.

And with that the two vile villains took off towards the kiosk to spend the afternoon sleeping in the bottom of the popcorn machine where it was nice and snug.

Jasper looked around the gloomy drain. The walls were covered with slime, the floor was thick with fungus and the rubbish reached the roof.

But worst of all was the terrible stink coming from
a pile of lice-infested underpants in the corner.

Poor Jasper! He missed the lilly-pilly tree and his
lovely leafy home.

He rattled the steel grate. It was locked tight.

Back at the fountain, the soup
Pearlie had made was stone cold
and she was still waiting for
Jasper to return. She
thought he might be lost.

Pearlie flew through the park looking
everywhere for Jasper
and then she heard
him call.

'Help, help! I'm being held prisoner!'

'Jasper?' Pearlie looked through the bars into the gloomy drain. The little elf told his new friend Pearlie everything that had happened.

'I'll use my magic to set you free. Then I will find those rats and punish them,' said Pearlie crossly.

'No . . . wait,' said Jasper. 'Those mean rodent dudes will be back. I have a plan to give them the fright of their lives.'

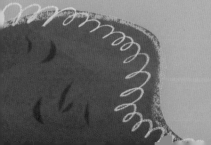

Now Pearlie knew that
although elves could not
do magic, they were very
clever indeed, so she hid
in a nearby bush to watch
the fun.

Sure enough, Scrag and Mr Flea were soon back with their bellies full of popcorn.

'After he's cleaned the house, we'll make him cook our dinner,' laughed Scrag.

'Clean undies . . . sensational,' chuckled Mr Flea.

The rats unlocked their front door.

In a flash Jasper somersaulted out on top of them. His ropes of hair flew out in all directions from under his knitted hat.

'RWOAAAARRR,' he bellowed.

'EEEEKKKK . . . a giant, hairy spider!' screeched Scrag and Mr Flea.

They got a tremendous shock and sped off as fast as their bony rat legs could go.

Pearlie and Jasper laughed and laughed.

'Come to my place Jasper,' said Pearlie, giving him a hug. 'I'll make some rose petal muffins.'

'Sweet,' said Jasper.

'Yes, they are,' giggled Pearlie.

They were flying back to
Pearlie's shell when Jasper spied
an old iron letterbox by the side
gate. It had not been used for
many years.

He flew over and peeped inside.
It was clean and dry. It was
warm and safe. It was the
perfect house for an elf. Jasper
had found a new home at last!

All that afternoon Pearlie helped Jasper get his house in order.

Then all the animals in the park kindly dropped by with a housewarming gift.

There was a cobweb hammock from Silky and
Sulky, a downy feather sofa from Mother Duck,
some new snail furniture from the four frogs,
and a charming set of gumnut cups from Brush
and Sugar Possum.

Jasper's new home looked a picture. Most of all
Pearlie liked the painting of the lilly-pilly tree he
had made on one wall. 'It's really cool,' she said.

'Hey man, would you like a blanket?' Jasper
laughed.

Pearlie and Jasper shared a delicious supper of muffins and dandelion tea in his snug letterbox. Although it was a rainy winter's night, Pearlie felt warm. Her new friendship had made the sun come out deep inside her heart.